UNICORN DREAMS

A Creative Coloring Adventure
with Enchanting Unicorn Art

by The Coloring Girl

© Copyright 2023 The Coloring Girl, All Rights Reserved

Published by The Coloring Girl, 2023

Unicorn Dreamscapes is for personal use only and may not
be reproduced or distributed without written permission.

Email: Hello@TheColoringGirl.com

A note from The Coloring Girl:

Thank you for choosing this coloring book. It's an honor to share my creativity with you, and I hope that it brings you as much joy and relaxation as it has brought me during the creation process.

Coloring is a therapeutic activity that can help alleviate stress, promote mindfulness, and enhance creativity. It's a simple pleasure that can have a profound impact on your overall well-being. With this book, I hope to provide you with a space to unwind, to tap into your imagination, and to express yourself through color.

As you color through these pages, take a moment to appreciate the beauty around you, both in the images you're creating and in the world outside. Let this book be a source of inspiration, a way to connect with yourself, and a reminder to prioritize self-care.

Thank you for embarking on this creative journey with me. I hope that this book brings you a sense of peace and that the benefits of coloring stay with you long after you've completed the final page.

Warmly,
The Coloring Girl

Dedication

Honestly, this project is dedicated to my future self.

May she get where she's trying to go.

And to you. Because if you purchased this book, you helped her take one more step in the right direction. **Thank you**. Thank you for supporting our small business. With every contribution, **you're making our dreams come true**.

Color to your heart's content! We've designed the back side of each page in this coloring book to be intentionally blank, so you can color with your favorite markers without worrying about bleeding through to the back side.

Happy coloring!

Color to your heart's content! We've designed the back side of each page in this coloring book to be intentionally blank, so you can color with your favorite markers without worrying about bleeding through to the back side.

Happy coloring!

Tip: Utilize these blank pages for fun doodles, color testing, brainstorming or journaling.

BONUS PAGE

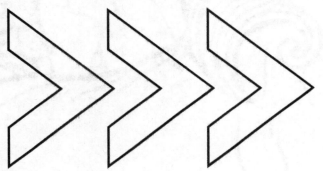

Dear Creative,

Thank you for embarking on this creative journey with Unicorn Dreamscapes! We hope this coloring experience has inspired your creativity and helped you find moments of peace and relaxation.

We would love to stay connected with you and keep you updated on future coloring book releases. Be sure to follow us on our social media channels for sneak peeks, behind-the-scenes content, and more.

Remember, the act of creating art is a beautiful and fulfilling journey. Each stroke of color on these pages is a reflection of your unique creativity and imagination. Keep exploring, experimenting, and creating. The world needs your art!

Thank you again for supporting our small business and happy coloring!

All my love,

The Coloring Girl

When you finish a coloring piece, snap a pic and tag us on your socials for a chance to be featured on our channels!

    @TheOGColoringGirl

 @OGColoringGirl

 Hello@TheColoringGirl.com

Made with ♡ by The Coloring Girl